Autumn
Publishing

Moana was a little girl who lived with her family on the island of Motunui. Her home was a beautiful place, surrounded by a coral reef and shimmering seas. Moana's father, Tui, was the chief of the island.

Little Moana loved listening to Gramma Tala's stories – especially the ones about the mother island, Te Fiti, which was stolen by a demigod called Maui. As he tried to escape, a demon called Te Kā attacked him and the heart was lost in the ocean.

"But one day," added Gramma Tala, "the heart will be found by someone who would find Maui, deliver him across the ocean to restore Te Fiti's heart, and save us all."

Later that day, Moana followed a trail of shells along the shore. Suddenly, the ocean magically parted and she saw a small stone with a spiral on it. Moana grasped it.

Just then, Chief Tui arrived. The ocean quickly whisked Moana back to the shore and she dropped the stone as Tui took her back to the village.

The years passed and, when Moana was 16 years old, her father took her to the island's highest mountain.

"One day," said Tui, "you will be the next chief of Motunui."

Moana wanted to make her father proud, but she couldn't help wondering what might be out there, beyond the reef.

Later, Moana saw Gramma, who took her to a secret cave. Inside, Moana gasped in amazement. It was filled with sailing boats. The boats belonged to her ancestors – they had been voyagers!

Gramma Tala told Moana the great darkness made the ocean too dangerous to sail, and so her ancestors forbid voyaging.

She then revealed the same spiral stone Moana had dropped all those years ago and told Moana she had to find Maui and restore the heart of Te Fiti.

A little while later, Gramma Tala soon became very sick.
With the last of her strength, she whispered to Moana, "Go."
Moana sailed past the reef, but a storm rose up. WHAM! A
giant wave crashed on top of her and everything went black.
When Moana finally woke up, she was on a strange island.

Moana heard someone approaching – it was Maui!

She wanted him to come with her to restore Te Fiti's heart, but Maui refused. He wanted to find his magical fishhook. The hook gave him the power to shapeshift into different animals.

Maui threw Moana into a dark cave and took her boat to search for his hook.

Moana escaped from the cave and dived into the sea just as Maui set sail.

Suddenly, the ocean pulled Moana through the water and put her back on the boat. "You will give back the heart!" Moana said in her bravest voice.

But Maui still refused to help her.

As Moana and Maui argued, they were attacked by Kakamora – little creatures dressed in coconut armour.

They escaped and Maui finally agreed to go with her, but still insisted he would need his hook.

Maui knew Tamatoa, a giant crab who collected treasures, had the hook and that he lived in the realm of monsters – Lalotai.

The next morning, they reached Lalotai and entered the monsters' realm.

The two found themselves in a dark cavern when Moana
saw the hook – and Tamatoa!

Thinking quickly, Moana threw the shiny heart of Te Fiti
towards Tamatoa, who scrambled to grab it.

Then, Moana opened her hand to reveal the real heart.
The giant crab had been tricked!

Maui grabbed the hook and he and Moana escaped
from Lalotai.

Using his hook, Maui transformed himself into a hawk and the pair travelled to Te Fiti. As they approached the island, Te Kā appeared and knocked Maui from the sky.

Moana caught Maui as Te Kā's fist slammed downwards to crush their boat.

At the last second, Maui raised his hook to block Te Kā's fist.

A huge tidal wave swept Moana, Maui and the boat far away from Te Fiti. Moana wanted to go back, but Maui's hook was badly damaged.

"Without my hook I am nothing," said Maui, before turning back into a hawk and flying away.

With tears in her eyes, Moana held the heart of Te Fiti out to the ocean and said, "You chose the wrong person."

The ocean then reached up and took the heart back beneath the surface.

Soon after, the spirit of Gramma Tala appeared, along
with hundreds of ghostly canoes filled with Moana's
ancestors. Gramma Tala asked, "Do you know who
you are?"

Moana realised returning the heart had always been her
destiny. She dived into the ocean and retrieved the glowing
spiral stone from the seabed.

Back on her boat, Moana headed back to Te Fiti. Te Kā
was determined to stop Moana and raised its fist, but just
before it struck, hawk Maui flew out of nowhere to take
the blow!

While Maui and Te Kā fought, Moana reached
Te Fiti. But instead, she found an empty crater and
the mother island was nowhere to be seen.

Not knowing what else to do, Moana began to sing the ancient song of her ancestors.

"Know who you are," Moana chanted.

Suddenly, Te Kā swooped down,
coming to a stop in front of Moana.
The young girl bravely pressed her
forehead to Te Kā's and placed the
heart into a glowing lava spiral on
the creature's chest.

Te Fiti slowly emerged from
the flames, with a glowing spiral
on her chest and a crown of
colourful flowers blossoming
on her head.

The mother island opened
her hand to reveal Maui's
hook – it was fixed.

The island exploded
with flowers and came
back to life at last.

Back on the boat, Maui prepared to leave.

"You could come with us back to Motunui," Moana offered. "My people will need a master wayfinder."

Maui smiled at Moana. "They already have one," he said.

The two friends hugged goodbye and Maui shapeshifted into a hawk and flew away.

Back on Motunui, everyone was overjoyed when Moana appeared on the horizon.

The young girl finally knew who she was: the next great ocean explorer, destined to lead her tribe on new adventures.